A tale of Moominvalley

PUFFIN BOOKS
Published by the Penguin Group: London, New York, Australia,
Canada, India, Ireland, New Zealand and South Africa
Penguin Books Ltd, Registered Offices: 80 Strand, London WC2R 0RL, England

puffinbooks.com

First published 2012
001 – 10 9 8 7 6 5 4 3 2 1
Characters and artwork are the original creation of Tove Jansson
Text and illustrations copyright © Moomin Characters™, 2012
Made and printed in China
Hardback ISBN: 978-0-718-19308-9
Paperback ISBN: 978-0-718-19309-6

MOOMIN
and the
New Friend

BASED ON THE ORIGINAL STORIES BY

Tove Jansson

PUFFIN

The autumn sun shone low over Moominvalley. Moomin and Sniff were down at the seashore doing the sort of thing they liked best, which is to say they were looking for treasure.

Sniff was humming quietly to himself, prodding and poking about in pools, when suddenly he gave a little shriek. "Moomintroll, come quickly! Look what I've found!"

And there, bobbing about in the water, was a bottle with something crumpled up inside . . .

Carefully Moomin removed the stopper and pulled out a twist of paper. "It's a message," he said.

"Read it aloud! Read it aloud!" squeaked Sniff, jumping up and down.

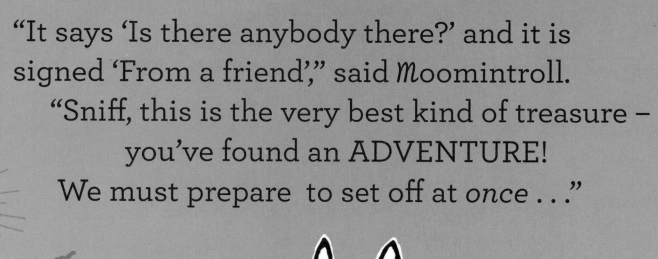

"It says 'Is there anybody there?' and it is
signed 'From a friend'," said Moomintroll.
"Sniff, this is the very best kind of treasure –
you've found an ADVENTURE!
We must prepare to set off at once . . ."

Back home, news of a mysterious friend was greeted with great interest. Only Snorkmaiden didn't think the expedition was a good idea.
"Why do you need a new friend, anyway?" she said crossly to Moomintroll.
"You have *me*!"

"Yes, and Snufkin, and Sniff," said Moomin cheerfully, "but a new one would be very fine! We have to go – it would be rude not to. Besides, they may need our help."

"And, anyway, it was me who found the message," said Sniff. "So the new friend should be *mine*, not *Moomintroll's*."

But Snorkmaiden didn't think that made any difference at all.

When things had been gathered and tummies filled, everyone went down to the bridge to wave goodbye. Moominmamma hugged Moomintroll.

"I have packed your woolly trousers," she said, "in case it gets cold."

Snufkin handed Moomintroll his rolled-up tent. "You may need it," he said.

"Mind you keep to the right side of the river . . ." called Moominpappa, but by then the little raft had rounded the river bend and was heading towards the sea.

The expedition had begun!

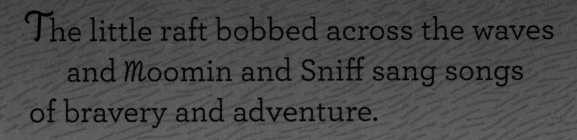

The little raft bobbed across the waves
and Moomin and Sniff sang songs
of bravery and adventure.

But as they were nearing Lonely Island
suddenly the weather changed.
The wind rose fiercely and the raft
was tossed wildly about.

And then,
   disaster . . .

"Hold on to the tent and swim, Sniff!"
cried Moomin. "I can see a light ahead."
The two friends battled against the waves
and swam towards the shore.

"But that's *my* message!" exclaimed Too-Ticky. "What a wonder! The first I've ever sent, and here *you* are!"

"But *why* did you send it?" said Sniff. "Do you need rescuing?"

"Hmmm, perhaps I do," said Too-Ticky. "I've spent the whole summer on the island. Winter on the mainland could be just the thing!"

As they scrambled from the water, a strong, comforting voice greeted them above the wind. "Moomintroll, is that you? What a night to be out!"

"Too-Ticky!" shouted Moomin.

Happily he introduced Sniff and explained they were on an expedition. Then he showed Too-Ticky the message in the bottle.

"But how will we get there now that the raft is gone?" asked Moomin. He suddenly felt anxious – what if he never saw Moominmamma and Snorkmaiden again?

"In the morning we'll make a plan," said Too-Ticky matter-of-factly. "You'll see. All will be well."

The next morning, Moomin woke early with a sense of excitement. "Pee-hoo!" he whispered under his breath, and he went to find Sniff and Too-Ticky.

Sniff was dancing up and down on the seashore. "Moomintroll, come and see! The storm has brought us presents."

It was true! The beach was littered with wonderful things.

Too-Ticky was busy sorting through a toolbox.
"We're going to build a boat," she said cheerily.
"The sea has given us just what we need.
Sniff's even found a ship's compass!
We'll use the tent for sails,
and we'll need a flag too . . ."

They worked and worked, and soon the boat was built. All it needed was a lick of paint and to be given a name.

"I think we should call it *The New Friend*," said Sniff solemnly. "In honour of *us*, Too-Ticky."

"That's a fine name," agreed Moomintroll. And he painted it in large letters for all to see.

It was time to set sail for home!

The New Friend

Back in Moominvalley, everyone was waiting anxiously for Moomin and Sniff to return.

"Moominmamma," said Snorkmaiden, "what if Moomintroll likes his new friend so much he doesn't come back? What if he's forgotten all about *me*?"

"Wait!" Moominpappa shouted. "There's something on the horizon! It's a whole ship not a raft, but I think I see Moomin's woolly trousers blowing from the mast!"

What a homecoming it was! Too-Ticky was introduced to everyone, and Sniff presented Moominpappa with the ship's compass.

"It reminds me of my days at sea . . ." said Moominpappa wistfully.

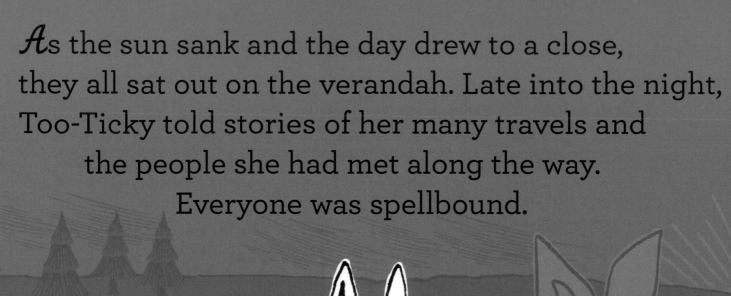

As the sun sank and the day drew to a close,
they all sat out on the verandah. Late into the night,
Too-Ticky told stories of her many travels and
the people she had met along the way.
Everyone was spellbound.

Then Too-Ticky was invited to stay
in the bathing hut, which she had
admired greatly down by the shore.

And one by one the family
                drifted off to bed.

Moomin and Snorkmaiden were the last to go indoors. "Look what I found for you on the island," Moomintroll said shyly. "It matches your hair." And he handed her a little golden locket.

Snorkmaiden blushed with delight and kissed Moomin on the nose.

"I'm sorry I was jealous," she said. "I like Too-Ticky. Do you think she'll stay long?"

"I hope so," said Moomintroll. "Would you mind?"

"No," said Snorkmaiden. "I did before but I don't now. It was just I thought a new friend would take my place and you'd forget me."

"I could *never* forget you," said Moomin. And together they went inside.

The End